THE EVENT

DANIEL GRANT

PART 4

ISBN-13: 978-1-948297-19-6

DALLENT

I0552735

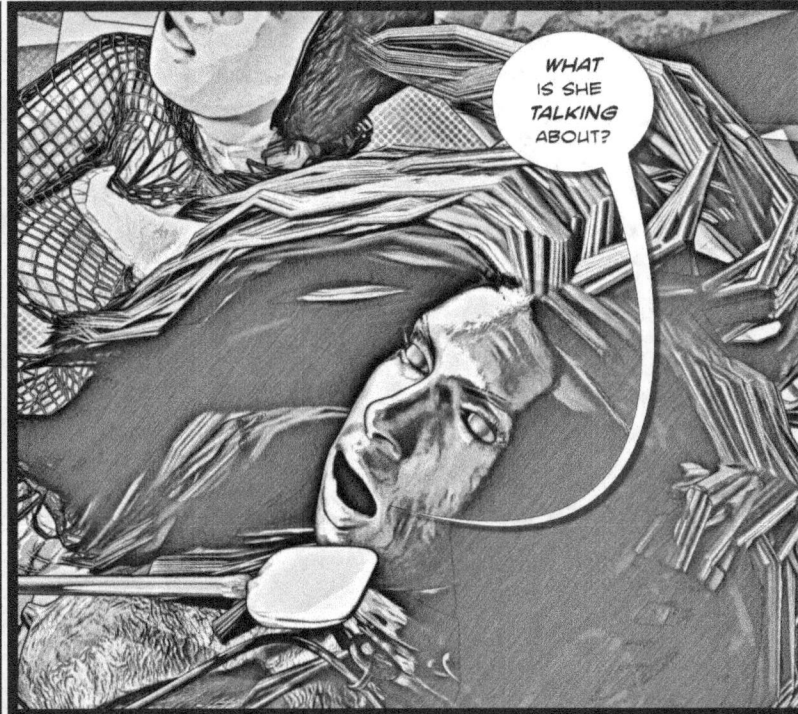

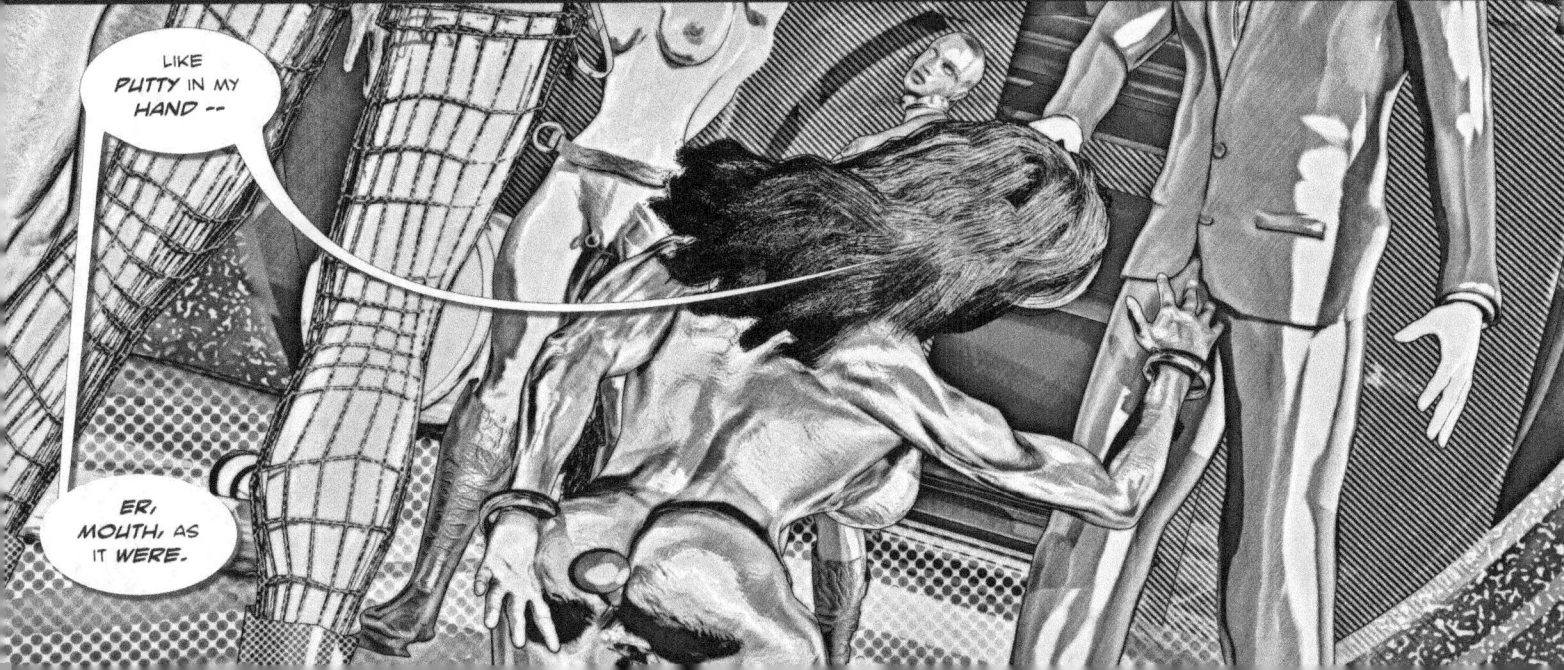

TROOPS, AND OTHERS, I'D LIKE YOU TO MEET CAMP INIQUITY'S FLAGS FOR THIS YEAR.

FLAG?

FLAG?

EVEN WE GET TREATED BETTER THAN THE FLAGS.

THANK, GOD FOR THAT, MAXIE!

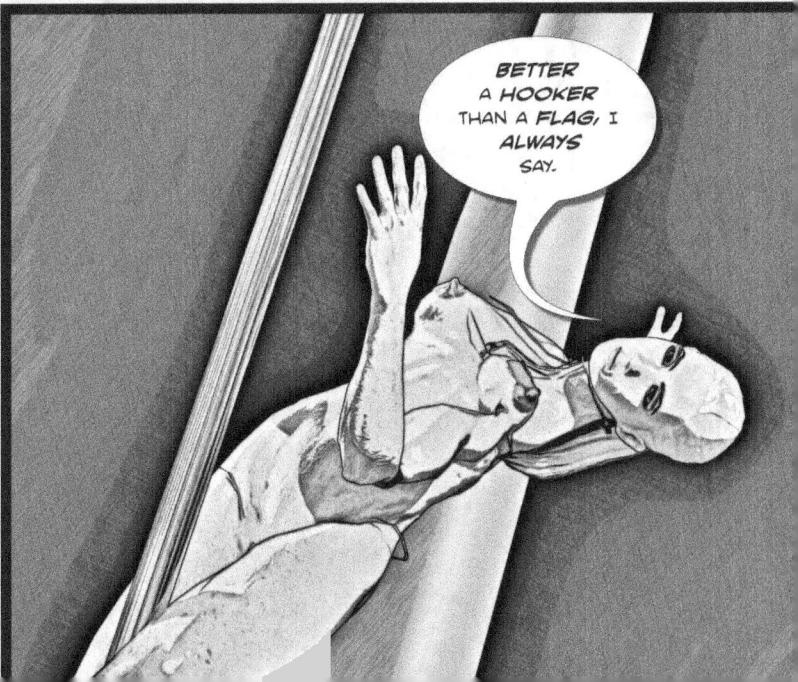

BETTER A HOOKER THAN A FLAG, I ALWAYS SAY.

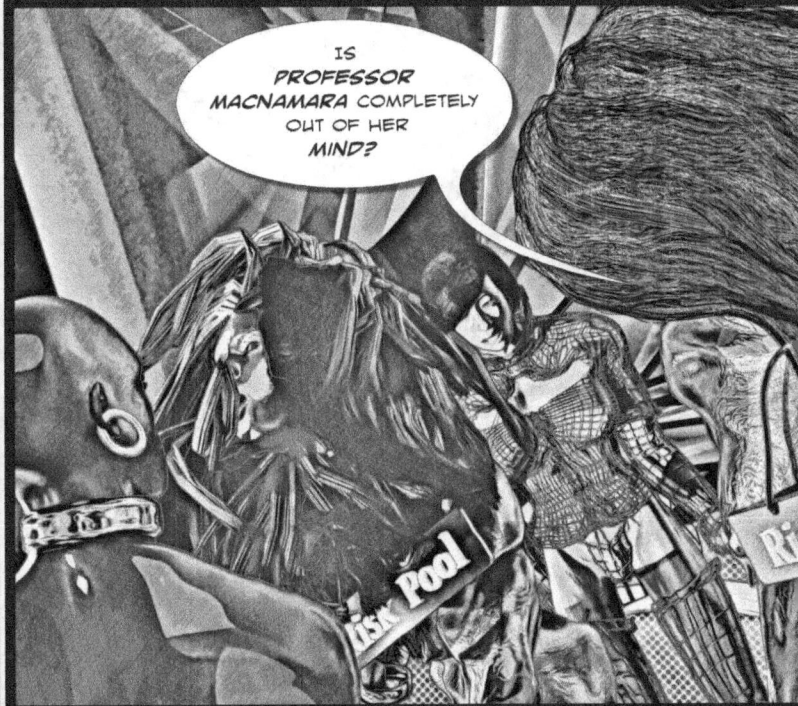

SMACK

SMACK

GRRR!

ARE YOU OUT OF YOUR GODDAMNED MIND, MILLY?

MY NAME IS GOLGOTHA, SLAVE!

OH, NO!

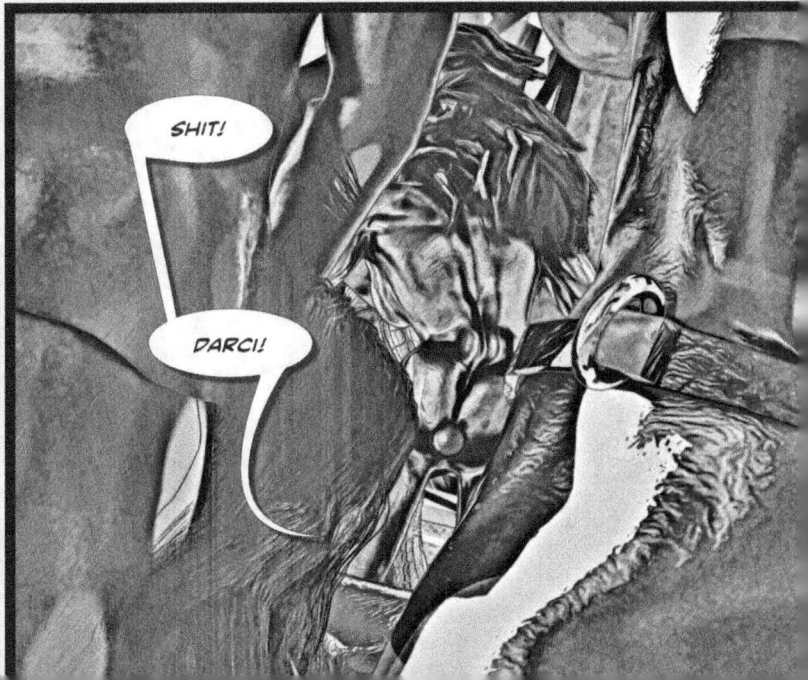

SHIT!

DARCI!

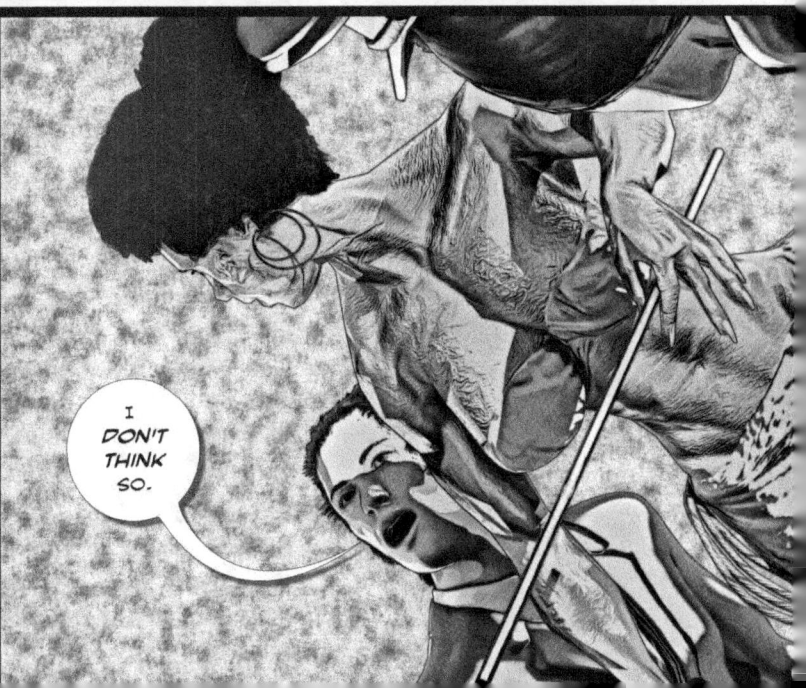

OHH

BAM

AHH

OHH

THUMP

DON'T EVER FUCKING TO THAT SHIT, AGAIN!

I THINK YOU'RE ALL BEGINNING TO SEE WHY DARCI'S MY ARCH-NEMISIS!

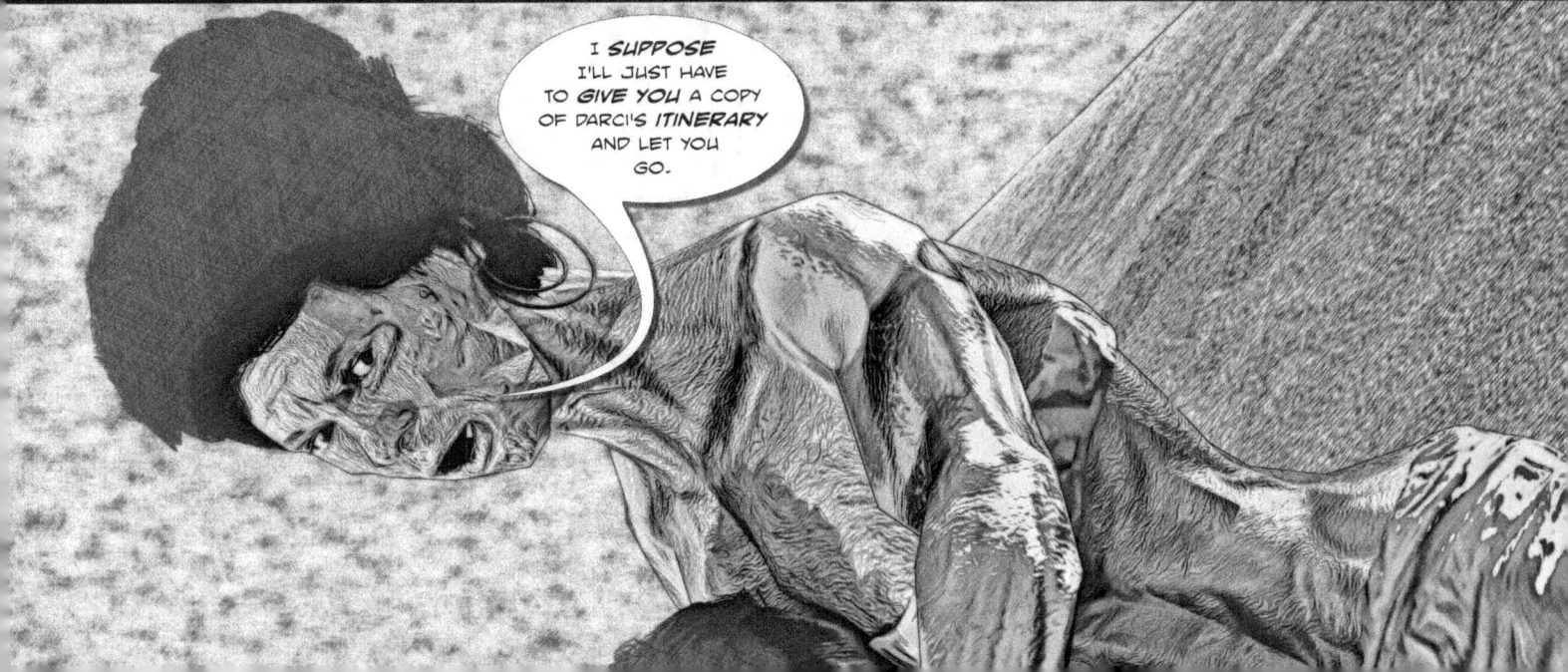

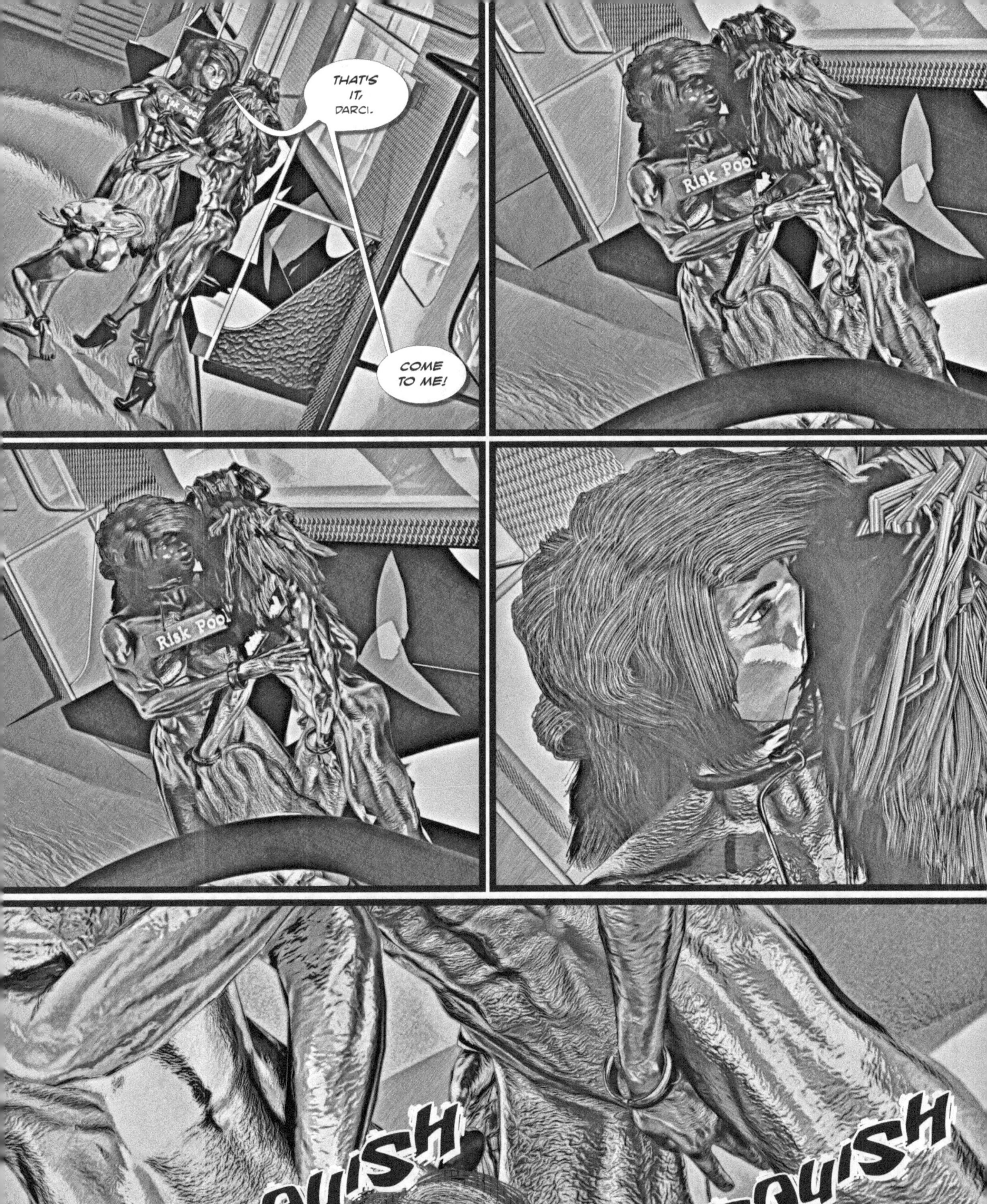

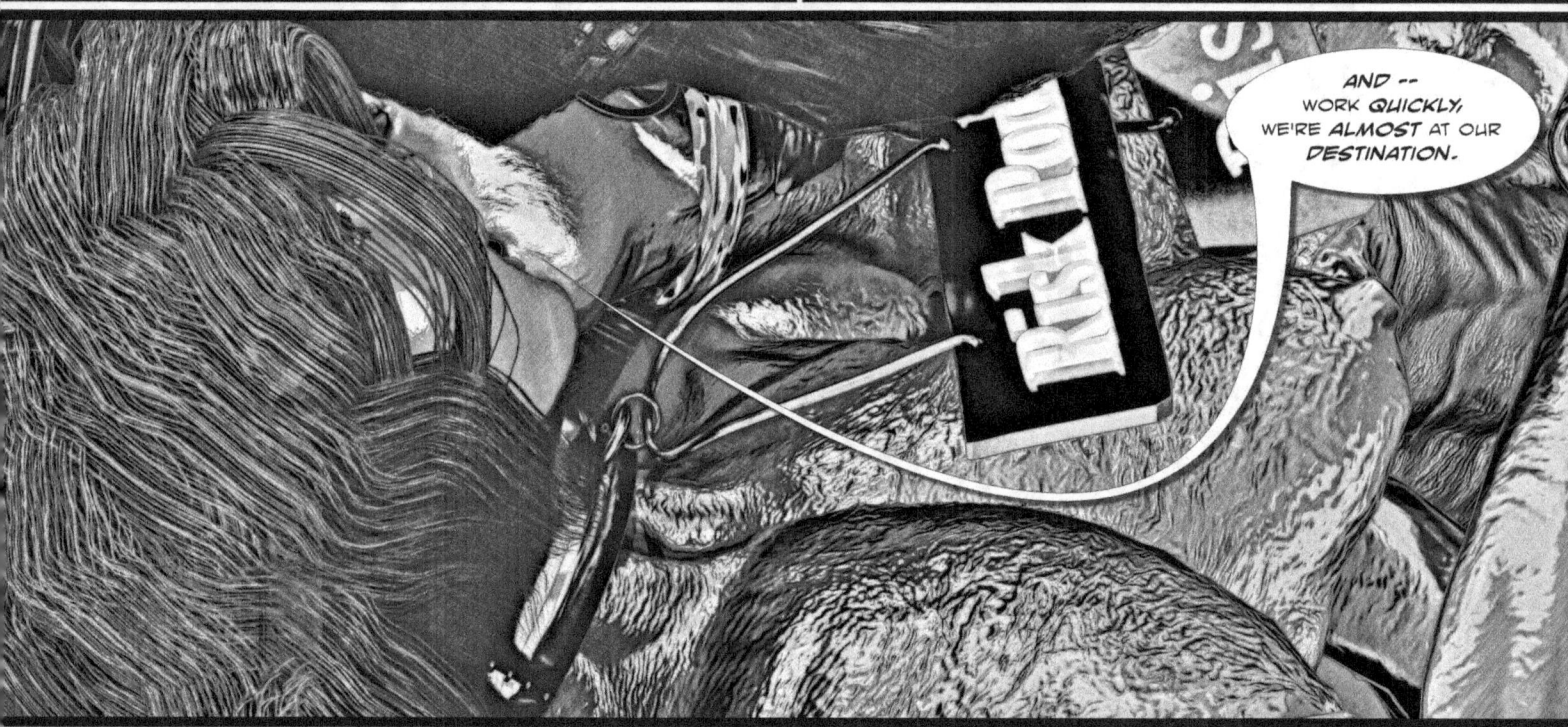

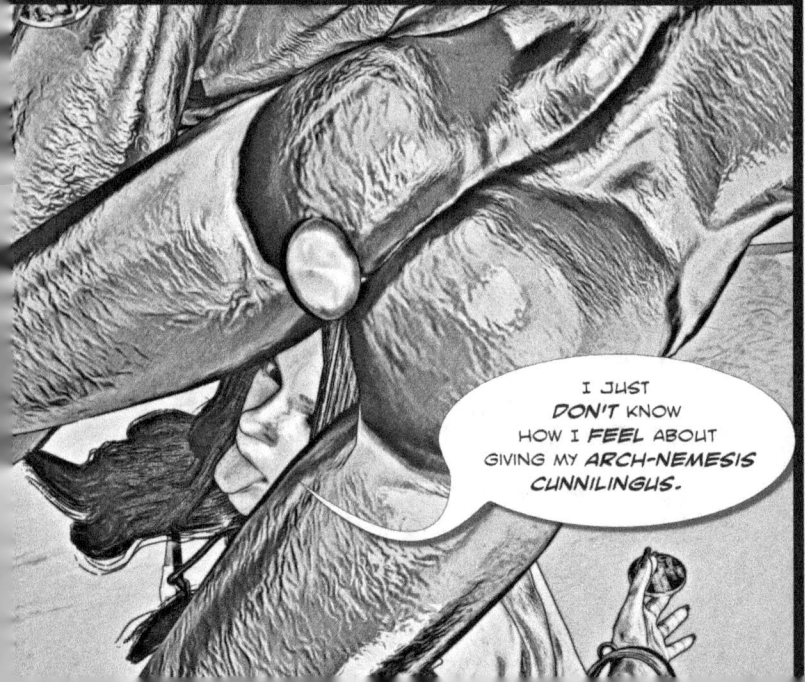